Antonella Abbatiello

The MOST
IMPORTANT
Thing

Red Comet Press • Brooklyn

One day, in a clearing in the woods, a **lively**

conversation began between the animals.

The rabbit declared:
"The most important thing is to have **LONG EARS**.
Those with long ears instantly hear any **tiny sound**, any **THUNDER** or *DANGER*, and can quickly escape."

"That could be true.
Perhaps it is so.
It could be **LONG EARS**,
but how can we know?"
thought the others.

"I do not agree," said the hedgehog.
"The most important thing
is to have **QUILLS**.
Those who have **QUILLS**
are **safe** and **protected**."

"That could be true.
Perhaps it is so.
It could be **QUILLS**,
but how can we know?"
asked the others.

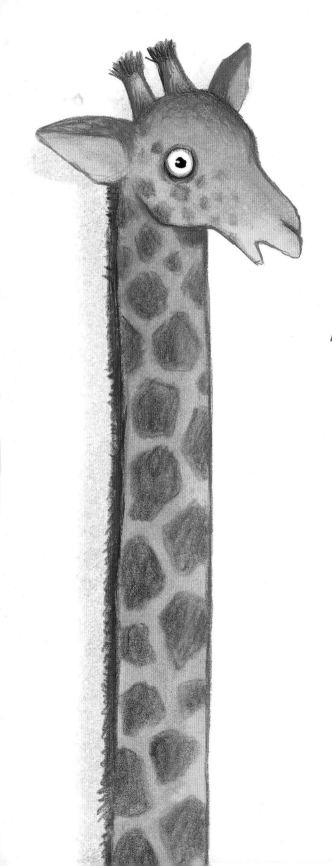

"It is not true,"
said the giraffe.
"Only those with a
LONG NECK can
reach the tender
leaves of the trees,
especially when the
grass is DRY
and the earth is **HARD**."

"That could be true.
Perhaps it is so.
It could be a **LONG NECK***,*
but how can we know?"
remarked the others.

"I declare," interrupted the frog, "that the most important thing is to be **GREEN**, to blend into the landscape and escape from **predators**."

"That could be true.
Perhaps it is so.
It could be **GREEN**,
but how can we know?"
wondered the others.

"For that matter," tweeted the bird, "the most important thing is to have **WINGS**. No one will catch you if you can fly HIGH in the sky."

"That could be true.
Perhaps it is so.
It could be **WINGS**,
but how can we know?"
considered the others.

"What are you saying?
For me, the most important thing
is to be **big** and **large**,
and to have a long,
beautiful **TRUNK**,"
trumpeted the elephant.

"That could be true.
Perhaps it is so.
It could be a **TRUNK**,
but how can we know?"
pondered the others.

"Without my **WEBBED FEET**,
I could not swim,
and the most important thing
besides **WALKING** is **swimming**,"

quacked the duck.

"That could be true.
Perhaps it is so.
It could be **WEBBED FEET**,
but how can we know?"
inquired the others.

"Absolutely not!" exclaimed the beaver.
"The most important thing is to
have **BIG, STRONG TEETH**
to be able to **EAT**, **defend** yourself,
and **build** a nice dam."

"That could be true.
Perhaps it is so.
It could be **BIG, STRONG TEETH**,
but how can we know?"
debated the others.

"Perhaps **ALL OF THESE THINGS** are important," hooted the wise old owl.

"ALL OF THESE THINGS?" questioned the others.

"Hmm, perhaps it is so."

"No, not **ALL TOGETHER,**
not **ALL AT ONCE!**"
corrected the owl.

"Each one of us
has something
UNIQUE and
IMPORTANT."

And finally, **ALL**
of the animals agreed.

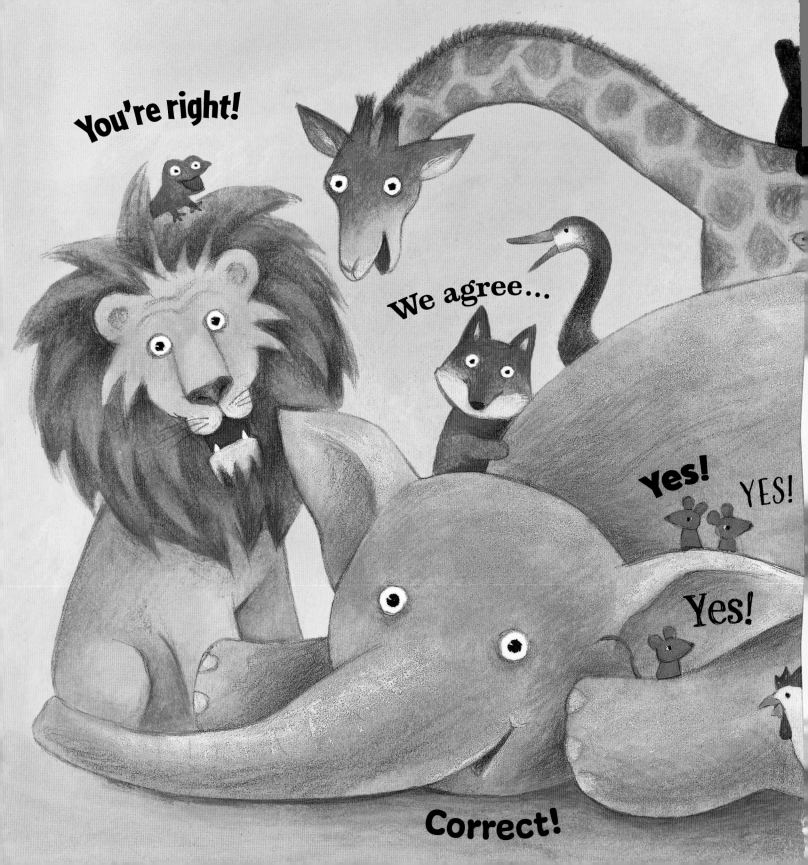

Antonella Abbatiello is a graduate of the Rome Academy of Fine Arts. She has illustrated more than ninety children's books, many of which she has written and illustrated herself. Her work has been published by all the major Italian publishing houses and her books have been translated into more than twenty countries. Born in Florence, Italy, she now lives and works in Rome. Visit her at antonellaabbatiello.it.

MIX
Paper from responsible sources
FSC® C104723
FSC
www.fsc.org

The Most Important Thing
This edition published in 2022 by Red Comet Press, LLC, Brooklyn, NY

First published as *La cosa più importante*
Copyright © 1998 Fatatrac, a brand of Edizioni del Borgo S.r.l., Casalecchio di Reno (Bologna), Italy - fatatrac.it

English translation © 2022 Red Comet Press, LLC
Adapted and translated by Angus Yuen-Killick
Creative Director: Michael Yuen-Killick

Library of Congress Control Number: 2021942831
ISBN (HB): 978-1-63655-022-0
ISBN (Ebook): 978-1-63655-023-7

10 9 8 7 6 5 4 3 2 1
Manufactured in China

RedCometPress.com